PRINCESS
LEARNS TO WALK

BY

MEEYAH JUJU

Meeyah Juju wrote this book
at the age of 8 during Covid.

princess is 5 weeks old.

SHE DOES NOT KNOW HOW TO WALK

princess tried and
tried but kept
falling and falling.

sHe almost
Got Hurt.

princess never
GOt Hurt Before.

SHe quit trying
to WALK.

Her Dad was suppose to be there but He was at the Doctor office.

Her Dad came Home and Princess was sad.

Her dad wanted to make her happy so He kissed Her cheek.

He sang her favorite song.

He made her laugh.

He helped Her get up and try again.

YAYAYA!

Princess learned HOW
to walk Because she
Did not Give up.

THE END

Made in United States
Cleveland, OH
08 December 2024

11552634R00019